FunkyYellowBus

Written by Robin B. Rosenberg

Illustrated by Bernie Freytag

"Don't worry 'bout a thing,

'cause every little thing gonna be alright"

Bob Marley

My name is Brookie Cookie
And I'm here to say
I have to go to Kindergarten
In just three short days.

What if I cry?
What if I fall?
Or forget my lunch?
Or get teased for being tall?

I don't mean to make
A big giant fuss
But please don't make me ride
On that funky yellow bus.

The day has arrived
I really feel sad
"Mommy, don't make me!
Oh, wait, is that Brad?"

Brad was my friend
From nursery school
We used to sing songs
And thought instruments were cool.

I took a big gulp
As the bus drew near
And went up the steps
And swallowed my fear.

I couldn't see Brad
Where could he be?
The big kids were loud
Somebody help me!

I don't mean to make
A big giant fuss
But I really don't like
This funky yellow bus.

"Brookie Cookie!"
I hear someone say
Could that be Brad
To save the day?

It was my friend Brad
Hip, Hip Hooray!
He's trying to wave to me
But he's too far away.

I don't mean to make
A big giant fuss
But regardless of Brad
I don't like this funky yellow bus.

The next day is here
I nervously wait
For the bus to arrive
What is my fate?

I step right on
Less afraid this time
I see Brad on the bus
And he's waving his arm!

"Come over here, Brookie!
I saved you a seat!"
I'm so happy to hear
He made my heart complete.

We sit together
With our backpacks by our side
Singing and humming
This is such a fun ride!

Until along comes Johnny
Who's older than us
What does he want?
He looks so tough!

But, boy was I wrong
He reached out his hand
He wanted to join
In our funky bus band!

I don't think I need
To make a big giant fuss
I'm starting to love
This funky yellow bus!

Johnny loves the drums
So he claps his hands
And gets us our rhythm
To the beat of the band!

He claps really loud
And very quickly you see
He gets others to join
In the funky bus melody!

Older kids, younger kids
And the bus driver too
Singin' and boppin'
On our way to school!

This is so fun
Our funky bus band
The key to its success
Was simply reaching out a hand!

I don't mean to be
In a big giant rush
But I gotta go catch
My funky yellow bus!

FunkyYellowBusEncore

The thing with music
You've got high notes and low
Sometimes it's fast
And sometimes it's slow

Melody and harmony
With a little beat
A beautiful recipe
That's always a treat

Music and people
Are one in the same
The very best kinds
Are unique and not plain

Colorful, happy
Upbeat and true
Makes the best music
And makes the best you!

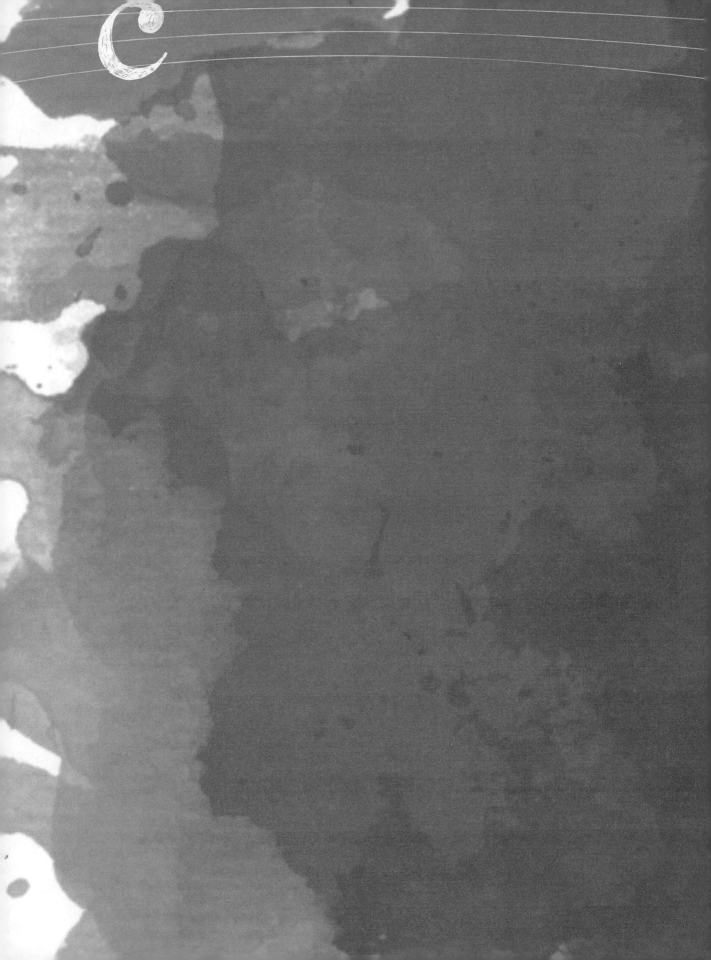

FunkyYellowBus

For more information about the folks who created
the words and images in this story, please visit FunkyYellowBus.com

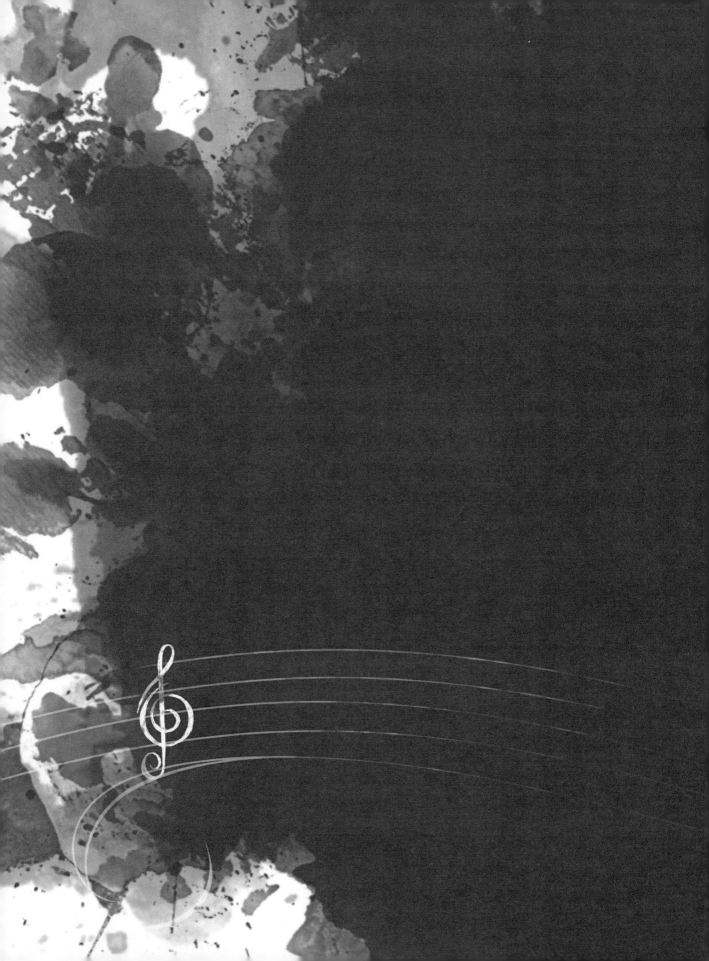

Made in United States
North Haven, CT
27 May 2022